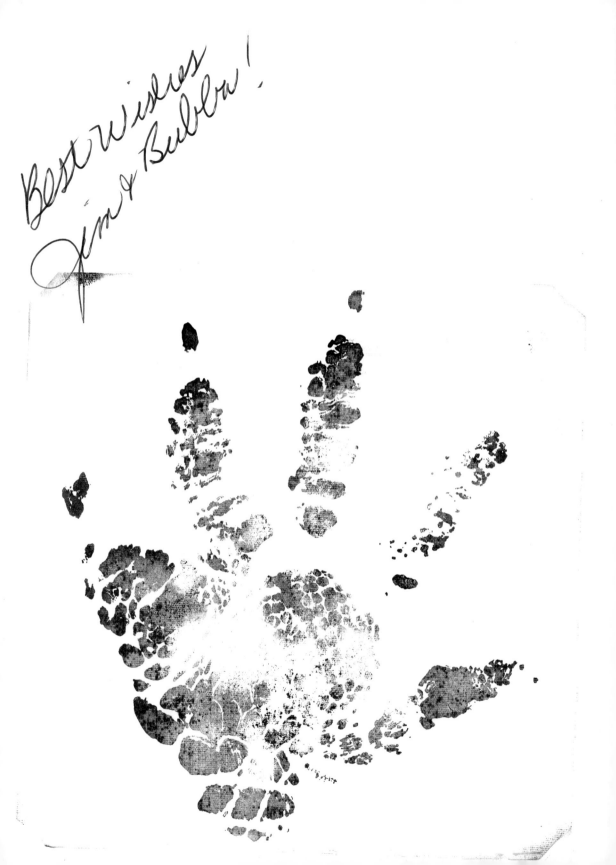

Best wishes
Jim & Bubba!

BUBBA

A TRUE STORY ABOUT AN AMAZING ALLIGATOR

WRITTEN by **ANDREA LYNN NESCI**
with **JIM NESCI.**

ILLUSTRATIONS by JASON KOSTELYK.

© 2003 by JIM NESCI and COLD BLOODED CREATURES.

ISBN   0-9713197-6-6

Printed in China

Copies available from:

Cold Blooded Creatures
website: http://www.coldbloodedcreatures.com
email: jimnesci@aol.com

FOREWORD

In addition to his passion for reptiles, Jim Nesci (owner/ handler of *Bubba* since 1991) is a dedicated husband, father and grandfather. Jim and his wife Linda reside in Homer Glen, IL. Daughter, Andrea, author of this book, makes her home in Lockport, IL with her husband Chris and two children, Cade and Carson. Son, Jim, lives in Naperville, IL along with his wife Julie and two boys, Payton and Austin.

As founder of Cold Blooded Creatures (Lectures & Presentations), Jim strives to conserve and protect reptiles by educating and entertaining his audience. While his love for reptiles was spawned during childhood in 1952, Jim's journey as an educator began in 1975. From classrooms to parties to television shows, Jim delivers a message to dispel myth and superstition about a very misunderstood group of creatures.

In describing the relationship between modern day reptiles and dinosaurs of the past, Jim sheds light on the importance of peaceful coexistence with all living creatures. To ensure the connection between humans and reptiles, Jim employs the art of hands-on learning during his presentations. Though Bubba, the 8-foot North American Alligator, is the true star of the show, the other reptiles, including a young alligator named *Lucky*, a large snake (*Blondie*), a monitor lizard (*Godzilla*) and a tortoise (*Tank*) provide an exciting representation of the reptile world. To quote the opening line from Jim Nesci's presentation, "Welcome to the world of Cold Blooded Creatures!"

DEDICATION

To a father who provided inspiration, a mother who nurtured my creative thoughts, a husband and children who supported me in every step of the process...I love you dearly!

BE SURE TO SEARCH FOR THE HIDDEN
REPTILES THROUGHOUT THIS BOOK!

Hello, my name is *Bubba.*
Very pleased to meet you.
I'm a North American Alligator.
Now let me tell you what I do.

I'm not just any plain alligator
that you'd see basking at the zoo.
I know what I do is special,
and I think you would agree too.

My job is quite simple. Through a presentation and demonstration, I teach children of all ages the importance of conservation.

Not an easy task for
an alligator alone.
So, next, meet Jim my caretaker,
who is also well known.

Together we go to schools, zoos,
birthday parties and charity events.
Some children have even seen us
at fairs under giant tents.

Oh, we're just getting started,
it's time to learn more about me -
The amazing reptile that
everyone comes to see.

Looking at all my teeth,
you might say I look rather scary.
But I will explain to you why
all my teeth are necessary.

My chompers are ready as I glide
through water searching for fish.
My long, broad snout enables me to
capture animals for a tasty dish.

It may not sound nice, but
just like you, I eat to survive,
and the cycle of life will
help keep alligators alive.

It was from the dinosaurs my
distant cousins that I've evolved,
and the mysteries linking us
have now been solved.

My prehistoric walk,
always gives it away,
that I once roamed the earth
with the dinosaurs of yesterday.

My back is heavily armored
with ridges for my protection.
So, if a large predator comes after me,
he'll think twice about his selection.

My legs are quite muscular
and so is my long, heavy tail.
Children are also surprised
when they see 5 fingers and
only 3 nails.

That is the way you see
I have evolved through time,
I was only using 3,
so I didn't need 5.

Many do not realize that
another amazing feature
is that alligators
are low energy creatures.

Small amounts of food
daily is what I need,
and because I move around
very little, it's plenty indeed.

When many first see me,
they're frightened by my size.
But my gentle nature,
always causes much surprise.

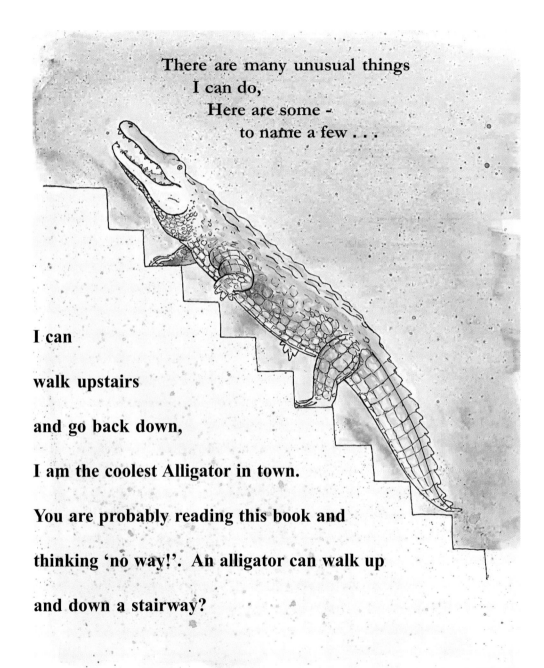

There are many unusual things
I can do,
Here are some -
to name a few . . .

I can

walk upstairs

and go back down,

I am the coolest Alligator in town.

You are probably reading this book and

thinking 'no way!'. An alligator can walk up

and down a stairway?

How many other alligators could give
children a ride on his back?
I do it all the time,
as a matter-of-fact.

'You wouldn't believe your eyes
if you saw me walking into my family van,
but once again, believe it because
I really do and can.

Another fact I would
like to share,
is that thousands of people
meet and pet me each year.

Jim has spent countless
hours working with me,
to mold me into a unique
individual that everyone comes to see.
We have a mutual respect for one another,
that is bonded with trust.
That is why listening to Jim
is most definitely a must.

It is very rewarding
to see children smile,
as they learn new
things about me, the fascinating reptile.
I may just be coming
to a town near you,
so, look for Cold Blooded Creatures
and you will find me too.

It doesn't take long
for Jim to dispel rumor and myth
and discuss why alligators
are truly a magnificent gift.

So now you know that I'm doing my part
by teaching you from an early start
that creatures like me should be treated
with care -
to ensure their survival in the world
we share.